THE SLEEPING BEAUTY

LITTLE SIMON

An imprint of Simon & Schuster Children's Publishing Division

1230 Avenue of the Americas, New York, New York 10020

First Little Simon hardcover edition December 2017

Copyright © 2017 by New York City Ballet Incorporated

All rights reserved, including the right of reproduction in whole or in part in any form.

LITTLE SIMON is a registered trademark of Simon & Schuster, Inc., and associated colophon is a trademark of Simon & Schuster, Inc. For information about special discounts for bulk purchases, please contact Simon & Schuster Special Sales at 1-866-506-1949 or business@simonandschuster.com.

The Simon & Schuster Speakers Bureau can bring authors to your live event.

For more information or to book an event contact the Simon & Schuster

Speakers Bureau at 1-866-248-3049 or visit our website at www.simonspeakers.com.

Designed by Chani Yammer

Manufactured in the United States of America 1117 PCH

2 4 6 8 10 9 7 5 3 1

This book has been cataloged with the Library of Congress.

ISBN 978-1-4814-5831-3 (hc)

ISBN 978-1-4814-5832-0 (eBook)

THE SLEEPING BEAUTY

Illustrated by Valeria Docampo

Based on the New York City Ballet production choreographed by Peter Martins,
after Marius Petipa and George Balanchine

LITTLE SIMON
New York London Toronto Sydney New Delhi

In a kingdom far away, a king and queen were celebrating the birth of their beautiful baby girl, Princess Aurora.

So overjoyed were the king and queen that they decided to throw a party in honor of their new baby. They flung open the gates of the kingdom and invited the entire land to celebrate.

Among the guests were Aurora's fairy godmothers, who swooned with delight over the baby. But one fairy godmother was missing.

The evil fairy, Carabosse, realized that she had not been invited to the party, and she was furious! How could she be ignored? What had she done to be left out of the festivities?

She fussed and fumed, her anger growing into fury. Then she came up with a plan. She *would* go to the party, and the king and queen would pay dearly for leaving her out.

The fairy godmothers were in the very act of bestowing their precious gifts of virtues on Princess Aurora when suddenly an electric current sizzled through the air. Carabosse had arrived in a chariot, enveloped in rage. "How dare you!" she roared as the court scrambled for cover. The king and queen realized there had been a terrible mistake: Carabosse had been accidentally left off the guest list.

But now it was too late, and Carabosse had come armed not with a gift but with a curse. "The baby will grow and grow and grow. But on her sixteenth birthday, she will prick her finger on a spindle and die!" she proclaimed. The entire court gasped, and the king and queen were beside themselves with horror.

Luckily, there was one fairy who had yet to give Princess Aurora her gift. The Lilac Fairy stepped forward. "Princess Aurora *will* grow and grow and grow, and on her sixteenth birthday, she *will* prick her finger on a spindle, but she will *not* die," said the lovely and kind Lilac Fairy. Everyone sighed with relief.

"She will instead fall into a deep sleep," continued the Lilac Fairy, "as will all of the kingdom. This sleep will last one hundred years, when she will be awakened by a kiss from her one true love."

The graceful Aurora grew up much loved and happy and totally unaware of the curse set upon her. For her sixteenth birthday, the king and queen planned another party, equal to the grand celebration of her birth. News of Aurora's charm and beauty had spread, and princes from all around the world hurried to meet her. Garlands of flowers were strewn throughout the kingdom as anticipation grew for Aurora's arrival at the ball.

When Princess Aurora glided onto the floor, everyone could see she
had grown into a lovely young woman. She took turns dancing with
all her suitors, and none could help but smile at the beautiful princess
twirling with such joy.

Guests had come bearing gifts for the princess, and among them was an old woman. Aurora had no idea that the old woman was really the evil Carabosse in disguise! Carabosse gave the princess a bouquet, and just as predicted, Aurora pricked her finger on a spindle hidden in the flowers. Falling under the curse, she immediately collapsed to the ground.

As the king and queen raced to Aurora, Carabosse threw off her cape, and the kingdom, realizing the evil fairy had come for her revenge, gasped in horror.

As the kingdom descended into chaos, the Lilac Fairy magically appeared. She reminded everyone that Aurora would not die, but instead Aurora would fall into a deep, deep slumber, as would they all.

As they drifted to sleep, a stillness fell over the land. Trees reached high
into the sky and vines crept up walls, covering the entire kingdom
and hiding it from the rest of the world.

On the exact day when one hundred years had passed, a prince named Désiré was riding his horse in the forest and stopped to take a rest. He began to daydream, and as he did, the Lilac Fairy appeared in front of him.

"You are thinking about your future," she said. "And I know where your future lies. It is with your one true love, a beautiful princess named Aurora." The Lilac Fairy showed Désiré a vision of Aurora, and he was immediately captivated. He just knew that this princess was his one true love, and he wanted to see her at once.

The Lilac Fairy led Désiré on a journey through the deep woods. They came to a lake, and there they found a boat. As they sailed and sailed and sailed, they suddenly spied on the far shore the top of a castle rising from the forest.

They reached the other side of the lake, and after valiantly cutting through the tangled vines and branches that surrounded the castle, Prince Désiré at last reached the beautiful sleeping princess and gently kissed her.

Just as the Lilac Fairy had promised, the kiss of Aurora's one true love lifted the curse. Aurora smiled and slowly rose, rubbing her eyes and stretching her arms and legs. She saw the rest of the kingdom restored to life.

How happy Aurora was to meet this wonderful prince, and how happy he was to meet her! Now that they had found true love, they agreed to marry at once.

With haste, the kingdom gathered for the royal wedding. Aurora and Désiré took their vows with love so strong it made the sunshine seem dull. The king and queen beamed with delight.

After their ceremony, Princess Aurora and Prince Désiré celebrated with a dance together. It was as if the entire kingdom had drifted away and only the two of them were left, as happy as can be.

While the kingdom continued to celebrate, characters from all the fairy tales, amazingly, joined in the celebration!

The White Cat and Puss in Boots sashayed and swatted.

A group of jesters performed tricks and flips, and Princess Florine
and the Bluebird floated and fluttered across the floor. The Wolf found
Little Red Riding Hood hiding in a forest of tree branches held aloft by
the kingdom's tiniest children.

The king and queen, so happy and relieved about all that had transpired, decided then and there that it was the perfect time for Aurora and her prince to be crowned the new queen and king of the kingdom.

The Lilac Fairy, who had saved
Aurora from Carabosse's evil
doom, blessed the couple and
wished them nothing but health
and happiness.

It was a happy day
for a happy couple
and a happy kingdom.
It was the start of a life lived
happily ever after.

New York City Ballet's
THE
SLEEPING BEAUTY
Fun Facts

- Upon Aurora's birth, 6 fairies bear gifts of virtue for the princess. (There is also 1 evil fairy, Carabosse, who was accidentally not invited and bestows a curse instead.)

- Princess Aurora is given 8 roses in the Rose Adagio, 2 by each of the 4 princes.

- Each performance features more than 70 NYCB dancers, 65 children from the School of American Ballet (the official school of NYCB), and 64 musicians in the NYCB orchestra.

- Each performance features 213 costumes, 54 crowns, and 65 wigs.

- The Lilac Fairy's tutu has 11 layers of tulle.

- The Garland Dance has 40 garlands.

- The Lilac Fairy's boat is 22 feet long.

The Sleeping Beauty was created by composer Peter Ilyitch Tschaikovsky and choreographer Marius Petipa, and it was first performed at the Mariinsky Theater in St. Petersburg, Russia, on January 15, 1890.

The ballet's story is based on a fairy tale by Charles Perrault, the seventeenth-century French author known for creating Mother Goose. Credited as the founder of the modern fairy tale for his stories derived from pre-existing folktales, Perrault also wrote "Little Red Riding Hood," "Cinderella," and "Puss in Boots," among others.

The Sleeping Beauty is the second of Tschaikovsky's three full-length story ballets, which also include *Swan Lake* (1877) and *The Nutcracker* (1892), and is one of the most popular ballets ever created, performed by ballet companies around the world.

New York City Ballet's production was staged by NYCB's Ballet Master in Chief Peter Martins in 1991 and is the most elaborate production in the company's repertory, requiring more than a hundred dancers, including students from the School of American Ballet, the official school of the New York City Ballet.

The Sleeping Beauty
BALLET IN TWO ACTS

Music by Peter Ilyitch Tschaikovsky
Libretto by Marius Petipa and I. A. Vsevolozhsky
after stories by Charles Perrault and others
Choreography by Peter Martins (after Marius Petipa)
(The Garland Dance by George Balanchine*)
Scenery by David Mitchell
Costumes designed by Patricia Zipprodt
Costumes executed by Barbara Matera, Ltd.
Makeup, hair, and wigs designed by Michael Avedon
Lighting by Mark Stanley

*© The George Balanchine Trust

Premiere: April 25, 1991, New York City Ballet,
New York State Theater

Learn more at nycballet.com.

Australian slang*

bonzer—*great*

fair dinkum—*genuine*

holy dooley—*good grief*

tucker—*food*

Look for these words inside.

DISCARD

Galahs and emu

Kakadu National Park

AUSTRALIA

Kangaroo Island

United States
Australia